In loving memory of my father, Noel Damon

Published by Peter Pauper Press, Inc.
202 Mamaroneck Avenue
White Plains, New York 10601
U.S.A.

Published in the United Kingdom and Europe by Peter Pauper Press, Inc.
c/o White Pebble International
Unit 2, Plot 11 Terminus Rd.
Chichester, West Sussex PO19 8TX, UK

Designed by Heather Zschock

Library of Congress Cataloging-in-Publication Data

Fraser, Mary Ann, author, illustrator.
  No yeti yet / Mary Ann Fraser. -- First edition.
     pages cm
  Summary: When big brother decides that a snowy winter day is perfect
for a yeti hunt, his little brother comes along, asking questions about the
mysterious creatures all along the way.
  ISBN 978-1-4413-0855-9 (hardcover : alk. paper) [1. Brothers--Fiction.
2. Yeti--Fiction.] I. Title.
  PZ7.F86455No 2015
  [E]--dc23
  2014040906

ISBN 978-1-4413-0855-9
Manufactured for Peter Pauper Press, Inc.
Printed in Hong Kong

7 6 5 4 3 2 1

Visit us at www.peterpauper.com

No Yeti Yet

MARY ANN FRASER

PETER PAUPER PRESS, INC.
WHITE PLAINS, NEW YORK

It's a perfect day
for a yeti hunt!

A yeti hunt?

Yup.

Why would we want to find a yeti?

To take its picture, of course.

Yoo-hoooOOO

Can it skate over slide-y,
glide-y ice?

Yup!

Can it see in a snowy,
blowy blizzard?

Yup!

Can it climb a slippy,
slopey hill?

What do you think?!?

I think you lost
your camera.

To thank him . . .